For Franklin & Olivia

BLOOMSBURY CHILDREN'S BOOKS
Bloomsbury Publishing Inc., part of Bloomsbury Publishing Plc
1385 Broadway, New York, NY 10018

BLOOMSBURY, BLOOMSBURY CHILDREN'S BOOKS, and the Diana logo are trademarks of Bloomsbury Publishing Plc

First published in the United States of America in February 2019 by Bloomsbury Children's Books

Bloomsbury books may be purchased for business or promotional use. For information on bulk
purchases please contact Macmillan Corporate and Premium Sales Department at specialmarkets@macmillan.com

Library of Congress Cataloging-in-Publication Data
Names: Wohnoutka, Mike, author, illustrator.
Title: Croc & Turtle / by Mike Wohnoutka.
Other titles: Croc and Turtle
Description: New York : Bloomsbury, 2019.
Summary: Although other animals are better at lifting, jumping, and running, Croc and Turtle discover something they are best at.
Identifiers: LCCN 2018024148 (print) | LCCN 2018024203 (e-book)
ISBN 978-1-68119-634-3 (hardcover) • ISBN 978-1-68119-635-0 (e-book) • ISBN 978-1-68119-636-7 (e-PDF)
Subjects: | CYAC: Ability—Fiction. | Best friends—Fiction. | Friendship—Fiction. |
Crocodiles—Fiction. | Turtles—Fiction. | Animals—Fiction.
Classification: LCC PZ7.W81813 Cr 2019 (print) | LCC PZ7.W81813 (e-book) | DDC [E]—dc23
LC record available at https://lccn.loc.gov/2018024148

Art created with Holbein Acryla gouache paint
Typeset in Delima MT Sd
Book design by Danielle Ceccolini
Printed in China by C&C Offset Printing Co., Ltd., Shenzhen, Guangdong
2 4 6 8 10 9 7 5 3 1

All papers used by Bloomsbury Publishing Plc are natural, recyclable products made from wood grown in well-managed forests.
The manufacturing processes conform to the environmental regulations of the country of origin.

To find out more about our authors and books visit www.bloomsbury.com and sign up for our newsletters.

Croc & Turtle!

The Bestest Friends Ever!

Mike
Wohnoutka

BLOOMSBURY
CHILDREN'S BOOKS
NEW YORK LONDON OXFORD NEW DELHI SYDNEY

Hey, Turtle. Do you want to see me lift this heavy rock?

Umm . . . sure, Croc.

I'm Croc,
and I'm the strongest.

clap
clap
clap

Hey, Croc and Turtle.
What are you doing?

Lifting this
heavy rock.

Can I try?

You can try,
but it's *really*
heavy.

FLING!

That was fun.

Hey, Turtle. Do you want to see me
jump over this big rock?

I sure do,
Croc!

I'm Croc, and I'm the highest jumper.

Yes you are.

Sure, but you'll have
to jump *really* high.

Hey, Croc
and Turtle.
Can I try?

That was fun.

I'm Croc, and I'm the . . . the . . .

. . . the . . . *fastest runner!*

Yay!
Go, Croc!

Hey, Croc.
What are you
doing?

ZOOO

Running *super* fast—
you'll never catch me!

OOOOOOOOM!

pant
wheeze
wheeze
pant

What's wrong, Croc?

Elephant is the strongest.
Rabbit is the highest jumper.
And Cheetah runs *way* faster than I do.
I'm not the best at *anything*!

sniff

sniff

You are stronger than *me*. You can jump higher than *me*. And you run *way* faster than me!

Wait a second.
Then that means . . .

That's not true, Turtle.
You're the *best* friend.

No, Croc.
You are the
best friend.

I guess we are *both* the best at something!

You know, Turtle, you are the best swimmer. Elephant, Rabbit, and Cheetah don't even know how to swim.

Actually, Croc, you have the best teeth. You have *way* more teeth than anyone.

Hey, Croc and Turtle.
What are you doing?

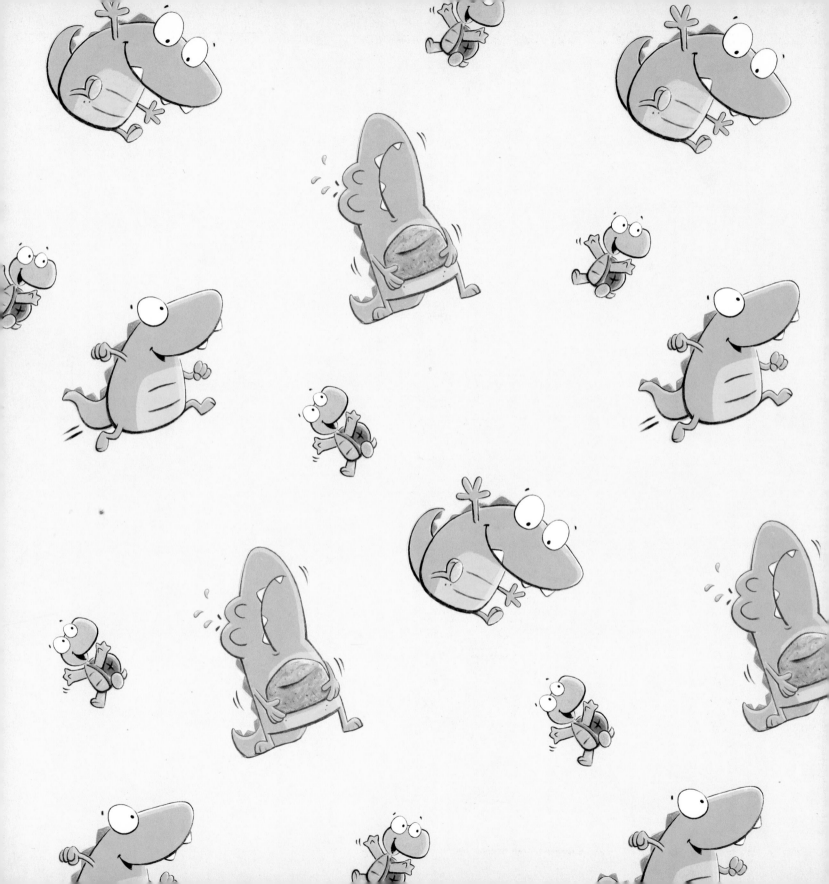